A Gift For:

From:

Published by Hallmark Gift Books,
a division of Hallmark Cards, Inc.,
Kansas City, MO 64141
Visit us on the Web at Hallmark.com.

Art Director: Chris Opheim
Designer: Ren-Whei Harn
Production Designer: Dan Horton

ISBN: 978-1-63059-684-2
1BOK1344

Made in China
0819

What Does a Big Sister Do?

By Delia Berrigan

Illustrated by Lizzie Walkley

Hallmark

A new baby is coming!

Have you heard the news?

You're going to be a Big Sister!

But wait.

What exactly does a Big Sister do?

She is the new baby's very first friend.

They will get to learn, grow, and play together.

They'll read stories and play pretend!

They'll get to go on all kinds of adventures.

You know, a Big Sister used to be a baby, too.

So she knows just what a baby needs.

Her parents will need her help!
Babies can't do a lot for themselves,
so parents are very busy.

Big Sisters can help feed the baby. Big Sisters can show the baby how she feeds herself!

She can help change and bathe the baby, too!

Big Sisters can show babies how to take a nap.

What else does a Big Sister do?

Most of all, a Big Sister is loved—

so very, very loved.

You are loved by all those around you

and especially by the new baby!

If you enjoyed this book
or it has touched your life in some way,
we'd love to hear from you.

Please write a review at Hallmark.com,
e-mail us at booknotes@hallmark.com,
or send your comments to:

Hallmark Book Feedback
P.O. Box 419034
Mail Drop 100
Kansas City, MO 64141